The Case of the Howling Armour

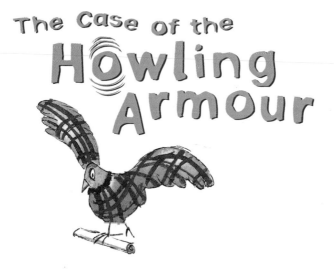

Sherlock Hound

Make friends with the most famous dog detective in town!

Be sure to read:

The Case of the Disappearing Necklace

... and lots, lots more!

The Case of the H🌀wling Armour

Karen Wallace
illustrated by Emma Damon

■SCHOLASTIC

To Rebecca, who always finds things out – K.W.

Scholastic Children's Books,
Commonwealth House, 1-19 New Oxford Street,
London, WC1A 1NU, UK
a division of Scholastic Ltd
London ~ New York ~ Toronto ~ Sydney ~ Auckland
Mexico City ~ New Delhi ~ Hong Kong

First published by Scholastic Ltd, 2002

Text copyright © Karen Wallace, 2002
Illustrations copyright © Emma Damon, 2002

ISBN 0 439 99446 2

Printed and bound by Oriental Press, Dubai, UAE

10 9 8 7 6 5 4 3 2 1

Chapter One

Sherlock Hound, famous dog detective, put down his violin and sighed deeply. Beside him his loyal friend Dr WhatsUp Wombat blew loudly on his recorder.

It sounded like a chicken stuck in a spaghetti machine.

Sherlock Hound took a deep breath and tried not to show his teeth. It was enough to drive a dog detective barking mad!

"How was that?" asked Dr WhatsUp Wombat hopefully.

"Once more," muttered Sherlock Hound.

ZING ZANG ZING

The violin sang
like a nightingale
on a moonlit night.

SQUORK
SQUEAK
SQUORK

This time
the recorder
sounded more
like a pig than
a chicken.

Sherlock Hound was about to suggest a game of Snap instead when something extraordinary happened!

A tartan pigeon with a message tube tied to its foot flew in through the window!

It opened its beak and squawked loudly.

Dr WhatsUp Wombat unfastened the tube and looked at the message.

HELP!
It's an emergency!
Come now!
Lady SquawkMighty

Sherlock Hound put on his special travelling cloak and a pair of warm brown trousers. "We'll go to Lady SquawkMighty right away."

"How did you know it was from Lady SquawkMighty?" gasped Dr WhatsUp Wombat.

"Easy peasy," replied Sherlock Hound. "Only Lady SquawkMighty keeps tartan pigeons."

Ten minutes later, Sherlock Hound and Dr WhatsUp Wombat were sitting on a train heading north to Scotland.

Chapter Two

SquawkMighty Castle looked like a set of
bagpipes made out of stone.

Lady SquawkMighty stood in the door.
"It's a disaster!" she squawked as she led
them into the Great Hall.

"My castle is haunted! Every time I play the bagpipes, I hear blood-curdling laughter!"

Lady SquawkMighty sniffed. "The SquawkMighty Clan hate being laughed at," she cried. "Now they'll never come to the Big Bagpipe Bop!"

Sherlock Hound looked serious. Every year the SquawkMighty Clan came to the castle to play their bagpipes at the Bagpipe Bop.

And every year, they put lots of money into Lady SquawkMighty's piggy bank.

Without that money, Lady SquawkMighty would be forced to sell the castle.

"Why do the SquawkMighty Clan hate being laughed at?" whispered Dr WhatsUp Wombat to Sherlock Hound.

"Because they are really **TERRIBLE** at playing the bagpipes," replied the dog detective from behind his paw.

Lady SquawkMighty wiped her nose on her silk tartan T-shirt. "You have to help me," she howled.

"When did you first notice the blood-curdling laughter?" asked Sherlock Hound.

Lady SquawkMighty pointed out of the window. "Just after that black and yellow submarine appeared in the loch at the bottom of the garden," she replied.

"There's only one person who would have a furry black and yellow submarine," muttered Sherlock Hound.

He picked up a set of bagpipes and handed them to Lady SquawkMighty. "Play something. NOW!"

Lady SquawkMighty blew as hard as she could. She sounded absolutely terrible!

Immediately a howl of blood-curdling laughter filled the air.

Ha
Ha
Ha

Sherlock Hound felt his stomach turn to ice.

"Just as I thought," he cried. "This is Professor Ha-ha Hyena! Master of disguise and the most evil criminal in the world!"

"What does he want?" squawked Lady SquawkMighty.

"The horrible hyena is trying to force you to sell your castle," said Sherlock Hound.

Lady SquawkMighty went purple with rage. "How CAN he?"

"Easy peasy," replied Sherlock Hound. "If the blood-curdling laughter stops the SquawkMighty Clan from coming to the Bagpipe Bop, what will happen to your piggy bank?"

Lady SquawkMighty's purple face went white. "It will be empty!" she squawked. "I'll go bankrupt!"

And she fainted with a THUD!

"What now?" cried Dr WhatsUp Wombat.
Sherlock Hound looked thoughtful.
"Play the bagpipes," he said, in a serious
voice.

Chapter Three

As soon as Dr WhatsUp Wombat blew into
the bagpipes, terrible laughter filled the room.

Sherlock Hound spun round. The laughter
was coming from a huge coat of armour in
the corner of the Great Hall!

He rushed over and pulled back the metal head. A black and yellow tape machine was hidden inside!

"No wonder poor Lady SquawkMighty thought the castle was haunted," muttered Sherlock Hound. "At the sound of bagpipes, this machine switches itself on and blood-curdling laughter fills the air."

Dr WhatsUp Wombat twirled his whiskers.

"Somehow we must trick Professor Ha-ha Hyena into thinking his devilish plan has worked," he muttered.

Sherlock Hound didn't reply. He was looking at a painting of the SquawkMighty Clan.

Sherlock Hound thought hard. How could Professor Ha-ha Hyena know how to ruin the Bagpipe Bop?

Someone must have squawked and told him how much the SquawkMighty Clan HATED to be laughed at.

Sherlock Hound moved his extra strong magnifying glass over the painting.

Sure enough, one person wasn't holding a set of bagpipes.

His name was DoughHead SquawkMighty.

Could he be the squawker?

"I have a plan!" cried Sherlock Hound.
"Fetch me a paintbrush and a wooden sign
and summon the whole SquawkMighty
Clan right away!"

Chapter Four

Inside his sneaky submarine, Professor
Ha-ha Hyena poured out a bottle of
extra fizzy champagne. Opposite him,
DoughHead SquawkMighty stuffed his
face with peanuts.

"More champagne, dear DoughHead?" asked Professor Ha-ha Hyena. "I know how much you SquawkMightys love champagne."

DoughHead SquawkMighty held out his glass. "I've never squawked, I mean talked, so much in my life," he giggled. "It's almost as if I can't help myself."

Professor Ha-ha Hyena's eyes glittered in a very strange way. "I love listening to family secrets," he said. "They're so useful, don't you think?"

He grinned and sipped his champagne. From the moment this idiot DoughHead had told him how much the SquawkMighty Clan hated being laughed at, everything had gone according to plan.

Professor Ha-ha Hyena could barely stop himself from howling with delight! Soon Lady SquawkMighty would go bankrupt and the castle would be his for ever!

He picked up his telescope and peered through the submarine's window.

What he saw turned his mouth into a huge sharp-toothed smile.

An enormous sign was stuck on the lawn in front of SquawkMighty Castle.

It said FOR SALE!

Professor Ha-ha Hyena picked up a sack of gold from under the table.

"Come, my dear DoughHead," cried Professor Ha-ha Hyena. "It's time for me to meet your auntie."

Chapter Five

Inside the Great Hall, Lady SquawkMighty
was feeling nervous. So were the rest of the
SquawkMighty Clan.

"What if something goes wrong?" squawked
Lady SquawkMighty.

"Nothing will go wrong," said Sherlock Hound. "When the professor sees the FOR SALE sign, he won't be able to resist."

Suddenly Dr WhatsUp Wombat rushed into the room. "Places everyone!" he shouted. "Our plan has worked!"

A moment later the entire SquawkMighty Clan disappeared!

Then Sherlock Hound ducked behind the huge coat of armour and Dr WhatsUp Wombat crouched at the top of the stairs!

Only Lady SquawkMighty stood alone in the room.

There was a knock on the door.

"Come in!" squawked Lady SquawkMighty.

DoughHead SquawkMighty skipped into the room, followed by Professor Ha-ha Hyena.

DoughHead couldn't wait to introduce his auntie to Professor Ha-ha Hyena, the new friend who had promised to put lots of money in his auntie's piggy bank.

Now no one would tease him because he couldn't play the bagpipes.

"Auntie," he squeaked. "This is Professor Ha-ha Hyena! He wants to give you lots of gold."

Lady SquawkMighty stared at the professor's pointed furry face. She had never seen anything so horrible in all her life.

Professor Ha-ha Hyena smiled and held up his sack of gold. "I'm so glad you've, uh, decided to sell," he murmured.

DoughHead SquawkMighty's mouth dropped open. "SELL?" he squawked. "That's not what you— Ow!" He yowled with pain because Professor Ha-ha Hyena stamped on his foot.

Lady SquawkMighty cleared her throat. "I'm so glad you've, uh, decided to buy," she squawked.

But as she put out her hand to take the gold, a look on her face suddenly made Professor Ha-ha Hyena suspicious.

It was almost as if she was expecting him!

Professor Ha-ha Hyena felt his nose twitch. Once to the left, three to the right.

There was only one smell that could make his nose do that!

HOUND! SHERLOCK HOUND!

It was a trap!

"The deal's off!" snarled Professor Ha-ha Hyena. And he ran for the door.

"Not so fast, Professor!" Sherlock Hound jumped out from behind the huge coat of armour and raised his paw. It was the signal everyone was waiting for!

Chapter Six

Suddenly a SquawkMighty jumped out from behind every curtain, chair and cupboard in the Great Hall, and blew their bagpipes!

The noise was TERRIBLE!

For a split second Professor Ha-ha Hyena couldn't think straight.

In that same second Dr WhatsUp Wombat dropped a huge heavy net from the top of the stairs.

SNAP! SNAP!

Professor Ha-ha Hyena's razor sharp teeth bit through the net before it had time to touch the ground!

Then he laughed a
blood-curdling laugh
and jumped out
of the window.

"Catch that
criminal!" barked
Sherlock Hound.

But everyone in the SquawkMighty Clan
was holding a bagpipe so they couldn't run.

Except DoughHead SquawkMighty, and
he was madder than a bumblebee stuck in
a bottle.

He ran after Professor Ha-ha Hyena,
grabbed him by the tail and pulled him
to the ground.

As the horrible hyena let out a howl of
pain there was a huge bang from the side
of the loch.

Dr WhatsUp Wombat had blown up the professor's sneaky submarine!

Now there was only one way to escape!

Professor Ha-ha Hyena dropped his sack of gold and raced towards the forest!

As he disappeared into the trees a tremendous screech filled the air.

It was the sound of the SquawkMighty Clan cheering!

Back at 221b
Barker Street,
Sherlock Hound
played a few notes
on his violin.

Beside him, Dr WhatsUp Wombat blew
loudly on his recorder. It sounded
absolutely awful.

Sherlock Hound was about to suggest a
game of Snakes and Ladders when there
was a knock on the door.

"Special Delivery!" cried a young man.
He held out a parcel with a note pinned
on the side.

Sherlock Hound
read the note.
It said:

Dr WhatsUp Wombat stared at the parcel. It was big and lumpy and looked just like a set of bagpipes. A hopeful gleam came into his eyes.

"My dear WhatsUp," said Sherlock Hound. He shook his head and smiled. "Don't even think about it!"